Jenny Greenteeth

RECEIVED MAY 1 7 2013

J FIC Jarma

Jarman, J.
Jenny Greenteeth.

THOROLD PUBLIC LIBRARY

PRICE: $5.89 (3797/jf   )

First published 2012 by A & C Black,
an imprint of Bloomsbury Publishing Plc
50 Bedford Square, London WC1B 3DP

www.acblack.com
www.bloomsbury.com

Copyright © 2012 A & C Black
Text copyright © 2012 Julia Jarman
Illustration copyright © 2012 Ollie Cuthbertson

The rights of Julia Jarman and Ollie Cuthbertson to be identified
as the author and illustrator of this work respectively, have been asserted by
them in accordance with the Copyrights, Designs and Patents Act 1988.

ISBN 978-1-4081-7410-4

A CIP catalogue for this book is available from the British Library.

All rights reserved. No part of this publication may be
reproduced in any form or by any means – graphic, electronic or
mechanical, including photocopying, recording, taping or information
storage and retrieval systems – without the prior permission
in writing of the publishers.

This book is produced using paper that is made from wood
grown in managed, sustainable forests. It is natural, renewable
and recyclable. The logging and manufacturing processes conform
to the environmental regulations of the country of origin.

Printed by CPI Group (UK), Croydon, CR0 4YY

1 3 5 7 9 10 8 6 4 2

recommended by
www.catchup.org

Catch Up is a not-for-profit charity
which aims to address the problem of
underachievement that has its roots in
literacy and numeracy difficulties.

Jenny Greenteeth

Julia Jarman

A & C Black • London

Contents

Chapter 1

Water Witch

Did I really see Jenny Greenteeth? Nadia asked herself.

She stood in the school doorway.

It was a wet November afternoon. Rain was pouring down.

Soon it would be dark. Nadia didn't want
to walk home past the pond in the dark.

Kev and Matt came out of the door.
Nadia hoped they'd walk home with her.
"Are you going my way?" she asked.
"No. It's judo tonight," said Kev.

"We're off to the town hall. Come on, Matt." Kev set off.

"Staying there all night are you?" asked Matt.

"I'm waiting for Lucy," said Nadia.

"You could wait all night then," said Matt. "Mrs C is giving her a proper telling off." He ran off after Kev.

Nadia hoped Lucy would come out soon.

She tried to give herself a telling off too.

Jenny Greenteeth is an old folk tale. A story. A joke. She's not real, she told herself.

It was true. Mothers told their little children, "Don't go near the pond or Jenny Greenteeth will get you!"

And the little children laughed.

So why can't I? wondered Nadia.

The pond was on Clophill Road, between the church and the pub. Green slime covered the surface. They'd done a school project on it last term.

When Matt lost his pond net in the slime, Mrs C had joked, "Be careful, Matt or Jenny Greenteeth will get you!"

Everyone had laughed. Even Nadia. But that was then.

Did I really see her? Jenny Greenteeth, the water witch.

Nadia wished she could stop thinking about her.

In the stories, Jenny Greenteeth would hide under the slime. When a child came too near, she would reach out with her long arms. She would grab her victim and drag them to the bottom of the pond. Then she would nibble them to death with her sharp green teeth.

THOROLD PUBLIC LIBRARY

Nadia looked back down the school corridor.

Come on Lucy, she thought.

It wouldn't be so bad walking past the pond with Lucy. Lucy never stopped making jokes. Sometimes, when they passed the pond Lucy shouted, "Jenny, are you hungry? Come and eat Kev and Matt, will you!"

The boys lived on the same road as Nadia and Lucy. They all had to pass the pond to get to their road. There was no other way home.

What if she's there tonight? wondered Nadia.

What if she's waiting for me?

Chapter 2

The Skull

Lucy came running down the corridor.

"Naddy, come on! Stop day-dreaming!" she cried.

She pulled Nadia's arm and rushed out of the gates.

The rain was pouring down.

"Come on you two!" called the lollipop lady. "But don't run!" She held up her lollipop. "You could slip on a day like this!"

She led them to the other side.

Lucy started to run again. Nadia ran too. Hopefully they'd run right past the pond.

But Lucy slowed to a walk. Then the rain stopped. *Suddenly.* It was weird. One second it was raining. Then it wasn't. And it felt colder.

They were getting close to the pond now. Nadia was glad when Lucy started to chat.

"Did I tell you about my great idea, Naddy?" chattered Lucy. "To go as *her* to the youth club disco. You know it's fancy dress?"

"Go as who?" asked Nadia.

"Jenny Greenteeth, of course," laughed Lucy.

Nadia didn't reply. But Lucy didn't take the hint. She kept going on and on about Jenny Greenteeth, and how she was going to make her costume.

"I know what she looks like," said Lucy.
"Kev told me. His granny saw her once. She
really did have green teeth, he said. Rows and
rows of them like a shark. And she had green
skin and long green hair."

Lucy put out her hands.

"Oooooh! Oooooh! Oooooh!" she
moaned.

Lucy thought Nadia would laugh.

But she didn't.

She couldn't.

"S-s-s-shut up," stuttered Nadia. "I know."

Now Nadia could see the white railings around the pond. She wanted to cross the road to get further away, but cars kept speeding past.

Lucy was still talking, but walking faster now, almost running.

Maybe she's afraid of Jenny Greenteeth too? thought Nadia. She had to run to keep up.

"Lots of people have drowned in the pond, you know," Lucy went on.

They were nearly at the pond. They would soon be past it, if they kept moving.

Nadia tried to keep up with Lucy, but now she had a really bad stitch!

"Lucy, slow down!" called Nadia.

But Lucy didn't seem to hear. She carried on walking.

"Lucy, I've got a stitch!" Nadia cried. "Wait!"

But Lucy was gone.

Nadia stopped dead. She had to. Right by the pond.

She was staring through the railings at the pond's green surface.

A splash near the edge scared her.

What was that? Did something move?

Was someone hiding under the slime?

She desperately wanted to leave, but she couldn't move.

Nadia tried to cry for help. Her mouth opened but no words came out. Her eyes were fixed on the pond.

It began to rain again.

Nadia tried to turn her head to look for Lucy. But she couldn't.

All she could do was stare at the water. At the huge drops of rain making dents in the thick green slime.

Plink. Plink. Plink.

Something *was* moving beneath the water. Bubbles broke the surface as if something was breathing.

Then she saw a bulge in the slime.

It was just like last time. Just like yesterday. It was happening again!

A skull was rising out of the water.

It was covered in green slime.

Empty eyes stared at Nadia.

The mouth opened to reveal rows and rows of little green teeth.

"Aaagh!" Nadia screamed.

Chapter 3

A Secret

It seemed like ages before Lucy came back.

"It was just a log, Naddy, covered with slime," said Lucy, as she pulled Nadia to her feet.

"Come away from the pond. It was a *log*, Naddy!" Lucy said.

"Then w-where is it now?" Nadia was still shaking.

"It sank," said Lucy. "Or floated away. That's what logs do."

But Nadia shook her head. "I saw her, Lucy. I saw Jenny Greenteeth."

"It's just your imagination, Naddy." Lucy took hold of her arm. "I'm sorry I mentioned that stupid story."

"I saw her," Nadia said.

"Let's go home, Naddy," said Lucy. She turned Nadia round and marched her away from the pond.

"Left, right. Left, right!" She gave orders and Nadia obeyed, like a zombie.

Jenny Greenteeth wants me, thought Nadia.

Jenny Greenteeth wants me. I have to go back.

Nadia's head was full of questions as Lucy marched her home.

Jenny Greenteeth took bad children. Jealous children.

How does she know that I'm jealous? wondered Nadia. *How does she know my secret?*

"Left again!" said Lucy as they turned into the road where they both lived. Nadia couldn't remember the rest of the journey from the pond.

Nadia's head was full of other things.
Green things.

I'm not jealous, I'm not, thought Nadia.
If I'm not jealous she can't get me.

* * *

Lucy stopped at Number 34.

"Here we are." She touched Nadia's arm.
"You're home now, Naddy."

"You can go now. I'm all right. Honest,"
said Nadia.

But Lucy waited till Nadia's mum opened the door. Nadia's little brother, Robbie, was by her side.

Nadia couldn't help smiling when she saw her little brother.

I'm not jealous, she thought. *I love him.*

He really was a lovely little boy. He was four years old. He beamed when he saw her. He looked like an angel.

She hoped Lucy wouldn't say anything about what happened at the pond.

Lucy sounded nervous. "Hello, Mrs Toms. Er… Naddy's not feeling too well. So I thought I'd see her home, but I've got to go now."

She shot off with a last worried look at Nadia.

"Naddy!" Robbie flung himself at Nadia and she gave him a big hug.

Things were fine. Better than fine.

"Come in, love. Quickly now," said Mrs Toms. "What is the matter now?"

"Nothing. I'm fine. Lucy was being silly. You know what she's like."

"Well, go upstairs and get those wet clothes off," said Mrs Toms. "It's nearly time for dinner."

Chapter 4

A Horrible Dream

Safe in her bedroom, Nadia couldn't believe what had happened. It was like a horror film. She must have imagined it. It was just her silly imagination.

Then she heard footsteps on the path outside. It was her dad. She heard the front door open and close. She heard his big voice boom, "Where's my boy?"

Not "Where's my girl?"

"Here I am!" cried Robbie.

Nadia went onto the landing.

She saw her dad lift Robbie above his head.

Like he used to lift me, Nadia thought.

She tried to be sensible.

I'm too big for that.

"Who's my big boy?" said Mr Toms.

"Me! Me! I am!" shrieked Robbie.

"Of course you are!" Her dad put Robbie on his shoulders.

It made Nadia feel sick.

Go away! Go away, Robbie, she thought.

She hated herself as the words came into her head.

She caught sight of her own face in the mirror.

It looked evil.

Nadia told herself to stop being silly.

I'm not a child, she said to herself. *I'm nearly a teenager. I did feel a bit left out when Robbie arrived. I do sometimes feel a bit left out now. But I do love him!*

She really did. She adored him. He was sweet and cuddly and he loved her.

She went downstairs.

"Hello Nadia!" Her dad gave her a hug.

"Hello Dad."

Her mum shouted from the kitchen,
"Dinner's ready! Lay the table, Naddy!'

She laid the table like a nice well-behaved
daughter.

She *was* a nice well-behaved daughter.

Robbie held out a chip.

She pretended to be a crocodile. "Snap.
Snap, snap."

It was one of their favourite games.

He laughed. "Again! Again!"

He loved her. She loved him. She had always wanted a little brother or sister.

Or thought I did. Till he arrived.

Till no one had time for me any more.

Nadia wished she could stop these thoughts from coming into her head.

"Eat up, Nadia. What's the matter?" asked her mum.

Nadia didn't answer. She couldn't.

* * *

That night Nadia dreamt of Jenny Greenteeth. The water witch beckoned her with a hand like a flipper. Nadia went into the water. She went deeper and deeper. The water witch's long green hair wrapped around her – tighter and tighter.

Nadia woke up with a sheet wrapped around her. It was very early. It was still dark. She was cold and sweaty and shivering.

It was just a dream, she told herself.

But she couldn't get back to sleep.

A voice in her head said, *Get up. Get up. Go to the pond. Jenny Greenteeth wants you.*

She wanted to go, but not in the dark.

As soon as it was light she got dressed. She wrote a note saying she had to go to school early. She picked up her bag and crept out of the house.

Chapter 5

Meeting Jenny

Jenny Greenteeth was waiting. Nadia didn't see her at first. She leaned over the railings looking at the water.

Nothing.

Then something went *swish*.

Jenny Greenteeth was out of the water.

She was standing under a willow tree, on the island in the middle of the pond. Her face was half hidden by its branches. Or was that her green flowing hair? A nostril opened and closed like the mouth of a fish. A hollow eye stared at Nadia.

The witch didn't say a word, but her flipper hand beckoned.

Words came into Nadia's head.

I know your secret.

Come on in. Come on in.

Nadia ducked under the white railing around the pond.

But when she looked up the witch had gone.

Where was she?

Nadia heard a splash. She stepped towards the water and peered in. A single bubble broke the green surface. Then another. And another. Nadia moved closer to the edge of the pond.

"I know you're there," she cried.

And there it was, in the slime. The bulge of her skull.

The sunken eyes.

"W-w-what do you want?" stammered Nadia.

She leaned even further forward and saw a flipper hand beckon.

Come on. Come on in, she heard again.

"I'm coming," said Nadia.

She went to take off her shoes and felt hands grabbing her. She looked over her shoulder.

It was Matt. Where had he come from?

"Go away!" She tried to fight him off but he wouldn't let go.

"Jenny, I'll be back…" cried Nadia.

"NO, NADDY! NO!" shouted several voices.

Lucy was there and so was Kev. The three of them were dragging her away from the pond.

"Don't be daft, Naddy!" Lucy had tears in her eyes.

"Come away, Naddy!" Kev pleaded.

They were determined to stop her.

But Nadia managed to finish her message. "I'll be back at four o'clock, Jenny!" she called.

By this time Nadia had her back against the railings. Her friends looked at her, and then at each other. It was as if they thought she'd gone mad.

"It's your imagination, Naddy." Lucy spoke firmly. "It's all in your head."

"You mustn't come here on your own," said Kev.

Matt said, "Is this some sort of a joke, Naddy?"

But she wasn't listening.

Something else had caught her eye. Her
school bag. It was by the pond. It must
have slipped off her shoulder. Some of her
books and her dinner pass had fallen out. The
dinner pass was in the pond. Her photo faced
upwards. Water had seeped under the plastic
so her hair was covered with green slime.

"I look like Jenny Greenteeth," Nadia said. "It's a sign. She wants me to join her."

"Don't be daft," said Lucy. "It's a wet photograph. Get it out, guys."

She gripped Nadia's arm. "Jenny Greenteeth is just a story, Naddy. You need to forget about this."

Matt picked up her bag and the books. Kev got the pass out of the slime with a stick. He wiped the surface of the photo.

Handing it to Nadia, he said, "You must never come here alone, Naddy. Never. Promise me you won't." His dark eyes looked very serious.

But Nadia didn't reply.

Chapter 6

Don't Go There!

Lucy stuck to Nadia like Superglue for the rest of the day. At four o'clock all three friends were waiting outside school to walk her home. They crossed Clophill Road together before they got to the pond.

Nadia didn't argue, didn't try to explain.

It didn't make any difference.

Jenny Greenteeth wanted her.

She'd go back to the pond some other time. Alone.

Tonight if possible.

But her parents had other ideas. They said Nadia had to stay in and look after Robbie.

Mum was going out to start the Christmas shopping. Dad had some urgent work to do in the study.

Nadia got Robbie ready for bed. She read him a story about a bear. Robbie cuddled up to her on the sofa. He smelt of shampoo and clean pyjamas. When she had finished he said, "I love you, Naddy."

She said, "I love you, Robbie." She meant it.

She took him upstairs to bed.

Once again Jenny Greenteeth seemed like a horrible dream.

It's just my imagination, she told herself.

The doorbell rang as she went downstairs. It was Lucy.

"Hi Naddy. I just wanted to say that I'm not going to the disco as that stupid pond witch anymore. It's such a silly story."

"Well, if you're not, I will." The words just came into Nadia's mouth.

Lucy shouted, "No! You're *obsessed*, Naddy. *Don't!*"

Robbie appeared at the top of the stairs. "What's a disco?"

Nadia said, "Go back to bed, Robbie. It's past your bedtime."

But Lucy said, "A disco's like a party, Robbie."

She came in even though Nadia hadn't asked her to.

Robbie came downstairs. "I've been invited to a party," he piped up.

He set off for the kitchen, to get his invitation.

Lucy followed him. Nadia heard her say his invitation was cool. Robbie said, "I've never been to a party. What's it like?"

Lucy carried him into the sitting room. She seemed determined to stay.

While Lucy told Robbie about parties, Nadia thought about her fancy-dress outfit.

Once they'd put Robbie to bed again, Lucy said, "Let's watch a movie, Naddy?"

But Nadia said she had something to do.

Lucy guessed that Nadia wanted to start making her fancy-dress outfit. "Don't go as that old witch, Naddy. *Promise?*"

Nadia laughed. "I was only joking," she said. But she started on the Jenny Greenteeth costume as soon as Lucy had gone.

Nadia's swimming costume was green. The logo said *NAIAD*. That meant water sprite. So did the name Nadia. Her name suited her. She was good at swimming, and used to go a lot.

That was until Robbie was born.

Nobody has time to take me now, she
thought.

She found some old green tights to cover
her arms and legs.

She found green paper and cut it into strips
for hair.

She found some green face paint.

She wanted to look exactly like Jenny Greenteeth. She didn't know why. She just did.

Real pond weed would be better, thought Nadia.

She could stick it on her face.

She would get some from the pond tomorrow.

But her parents had other ideas.

Chapter 7

Pond Weed

Mum looked worried when she came in. She had met a neighbour, who had seen Nadia near the pond the day before.

Her mum said, "You were under the railings. Why?"

Her dad said, "You're usually so sensible, Nadia."

They both said she mustn't go near the pond.

Nadia said, "I have to pass it to go to school."

"Well, walk on the other side of the road," her dad said. "It's dangerous. Keep away."

Everyone was trying to stop her. Her friends, her parents. Even the neighbours. All that week Lucy walked to and from school with her. Matt and Kev sometimes came too.

In the evenings her mum found her jobs to do in the house.

But Nadia waited for her chance.

It came on Saturday morning.

It was the day of the youth club disco. It was also the day Robbie was going to his very first party.

Robbie was excited. He was going as a
pirate. Nadia had made a costume for him.
She'd got a small white shirt, and cut up an
old pair of jeans. She put one of her dad's
handkerchiefs around his head. Robbie loved
his outfit and wouldn't take it off. He wanted
to sleep in it!

But now he wanted a sword too.

"I must have a pirate's sword!" begged Robbie. "*Please*, Naddy."

He went on and on about it. Nadia saw her chance. There was a toy shop near her school.

"Mum, can I go and buy Robbie a sword?" she asked.

"Of course," said her mum.

Mum would agree to anything for Robbie. She didn't even mention the pond.

Nadia stopped at the pond on her way home from the shop.

Mist hung over the surface of the water. There was no one else there. She climbed under the railings and crept to the water's edge.

"Jenny, please may I have some of your pond weed?" she asked.

There was no answer.

Nadia waited, peering down into the green
slime. But there was no movement. The water
was completely still. So were the trees. So
was the road behind her. There were no cars.

Everything was silent. It was odd.

There was no sign of Jenny Greenteeth at all.

67

Perhaps it was my imagination? thought Nadia.

But she still felt the need to ask to take the pond weed. And to tell Jenny about Robbie.

"I don't hate my brother," said Nadia. "I did hate him – just a little bit – well, not *hate* exactly. But I don't now. I *love* him. So you have no power over me."

At this there was a sound – a hiss. As if someone was taking a sharp in-breath.

It came from right beside her. But when she looked there was nobody there.

Leaning forward, Nadia lowered a plastic bag into the cold water. She dragged it across the surface until it was full of green, slimy weed. She didn't see the angry face watching her from under the water. She didn't hear the rows of green teeth grinding.

Chapter 8

Just Like Jenny

When Nadia got home, she spread the pond weed on some kitchen roll to dry. In the afternoon she took Robbie to his party.

It was near Nadia's school, so she had to pass the pond again, but again her mum didn't mention it. She seemed to trust Nadia.

Good.

Nadia's mum said she would collect Robbie at six o'clock. She and Nadia could walk up the road together. The disco also began at six o'clock.

Nadia didn't stop at the pond on the way back. She hurried home to start getting ready.

Her costume was hanging in her wardrobe. She had three pairs of tights. Green of course. Two pairs were for her arms and legs. The other pair was to pull over her head. She had cut lots of long strips of green paper. She sewed some of them to the pair of tights she was going to pull over her head. She was sewing the rest to her swimming costume but hadn't finished yet. Finally, there was the dried pond weed, to stick to her face.

But it wouldn't stick to the tights. It kept falling off.

At half-past five her mum knocked on her bedroom door.

"Come on, Naddy. Time to go. We've got to walk. Your dad's got the car!"

Nadia didn't answer. She didn't want to move her face. She'd just got some pond weed to stick to the tights.

Her mother opened the door. She stopped dead.

"That's *horrible*, Naddy. What do you want to look like that for?" Mum gasped.

Nadia muttered, "Fancy dress. Need ten more minutes."

Mrs Toms looked at her watch. "I've got to go. You must come as you are."

"I can't," snapped Nadia. "Go on your own."

Mum said, "It's getting *dark*, Naddy. I don't like you walking alone in the dark. Especially not dressed like *that*."

But Nadia didn't take any notice. After a
bit, Mum went downstairs.

Nadia heard the front door slam.

Nadia was so busy looking in the mirror
that she didn't hear Lucy come upstairs.

She didn't even hear her friend open the
bedroom door.

"What do you think?" cried Lucy. She was dressed in bright red.

Nadia turned to look.

Lucy's face went pale. "H-have you seen yourself, Naddy?"

"Of course I have!" said Nadia.

She turned back to the mirror.

Jenny Greenteeth looked back at her.

The skin, the nose, the eyes. Everything was exactly right.

"Take it off!" cried Lucy.

Nadia laughed and Lucy gasped. Nadia's teeth were pointy and green.

She had bought false ones from the toy shop when she bought Robbie his sword.

Lucy said, "It's not funny, Nadia."

But Nadia just laughed again. She pushed past Lucy and went downstairs. Then she put on her coat and opened the front door.

The wind was howling and icy cold.

"Come on," said Nadia. She took Lucy's arm. "Don't be such a wimp."

They stepped outside into the dark.

Suddenly two pirates jumped out of the darkness.

"Hi, you guys!" Lucy seemed pleased to see them.

It was Kev and Matt of course. Nadia guessed that Lucy had arranged to meet them.

They stared at Nadia.

She said, "Pirates must be in fashion."

She was thinking of Robbie.

Matt managed a laugh. "You look as if you're going to rob a bank with those tights on your head."

But Kev said nothing.

Nobody mentioned Jenny Greenteeth.

But they were all thinking about her.

They got closer to the pond.

Nadia said, "Let's go and say 'Hi' to Jenny."

But Lucy and Kev took hold of her arms.

They crossed the road away from the pond and marched her past.

They were nearly at the youth club when everything went mad.

Suddenly Nadia's mum was in front of them.

At first she seemed pleased to see Nadia.

Then she said, "Where is *he*, Naddy? Oh, I wish you hadn't got that horrible costume on. Where *is* Robbie?"

"What?" said Nadia, confused.

Music was blaring out from the building just ahead of them.

"WHERE IS ROBBIE?" her mum shouted. "They said you took him home from the party!"

Nadia shouted back, "What? You said *you* were collecting him!"

"They said you took him, Naddy. So where is he?" her mum went on.

She walked round Nadia as if she thought she was hiding Robbie somewhere. "Don't lie to me, Naddy. They told me you collected him in your daft costume! WHERE'S MY LITTLE BOY?"

Suddenly Nadia felt her blood go cold.

Someone who looked *just like her* had Robbie.

Jenny Greenteeth!

Chapter 9

Robbie in Danger

Nadia couldn't move.

Terror froze her. Robbie was in danger.

She was sure of it. She had to save him.

But how?

She caught sight of Kev staring at her.

Suddenly he grabbed her arm.

"Come on, Naddy," he shouted.

They ran back to the pond.

"Naddy!"

Nadia heard Robbie's shout as soon as they got close to the pond.

He sounded cross. She saw him as she reached the railing.

A street lamp lit up the pond with a dim yellow light.

Robbie was at the water's edge.

He was pointing at the plastic sword she had bought him this morning.

It was floating on the surface of the cold, green slime.

Nadia wanted to scream, "Leave it!"

But that might scare him. He might fall in.

So she climbed under the railing, speaking gently.

"Robbie, it's me, Naddy. I'm here. Come away from the water."

Robbie spoke crossly. "Why did you put my sword in the pond? Get it out."

"No, Robbie. No. We're going home," said Nadia.

She reached out to grab him, but with a sudden splash, he was gone.

"He's fallen in!" cried Kev.

There was no sign of Robbie in the water. Not a bubble. Not a ripple.

"Robbie!" screamed Nadia, and dived in.

Chapter 10

Into the Water

The cold didn't matter.

The slime didn't matter.

Only one thing mattered. Finding Robbie.

Deep under the water, Nadia swam
strongly, her eyes open wide.

Weed wrapped itself round her arms. Her fingers scrabbled in the mud. Her lungs felt as if they were bursting. There was a terrible pain in her chest.

But she kept going till she saw something white.

Was it an arm or a leg? Grabbing it, she pulled.

But it was stuck!

Something was pulling it down. *Or someone.*

She pulled harder. Harder. Harder still.

The pain in her chest got worse.

Nadia couldn't hold her breath much longer.

Finally, something gave way.

Robbie was free!

Kicking hard, Nadia turned and headed for the surface. She pulled Robbie with her. Her chest felt as if it was splitting in two. Her heart thumped. But she hung on to him and kept kicking.

At last her head broke the surface.

Hands pulled them both out.

Someone put a blanket round her.

"Is…?" she began. But she couldn't ask the question that was in her head. *Is he going to be OK?*

All she could do was watch.

Robbie's limp body was on the ground. Someone was pulling weed from his mouth. Someone started to count as they pressed his chest.

"One. Two. Three."

"One. Two. Three."

"One. Two. Three."

It seemed to go on for ever.

"One. Two. Three."

"One. Two. Three."

Nadia couldn't look.

"One. Two. Three."

"One. Two. Three."

Suddenly water spouted from his mouth.

An ambulance arrived. Paramedics put a tube in Robbie's mouth. Then, at last, Robbie moved.

He was alive!

"You saved his life!" said Kev.

"You were so brave, Naddy." Lucy hugged her.

Nadia's mum was holding Robbie's hand. She was too shocked to speak.

"You'll get a reward," somebody else said. "For bravery."

"I don't want one," said Naddy. "I've already got my reward."

But she wasn't sure she deserved it.

Soon the police arrived. Nadia told them everything she could. She told them exactly what she had seen and heard.

Later the police questioned Kev and Lucy and Matt. They also questioned Nadia's mum, and all the people who were at the party.

Everyone told the police what they had seen. The police listened carefully and took notes. Then they questioned everyone again.

They couldn't work out who had picked up Robbie from the party. A stranger. Dressed just like Nadia. Who took him to the pond and threw his sword in the water.

It was a mystery.

A few weeks later Lucy and Nadia passed the pond on their way to school. A digger was at work filling in the pond. The council were going to build a new bus stop on the land.

"So that's the end of that old story," said Lucy.

But Nadia wasn't so sure.

Was that really the end of Jenny Greenteeth?

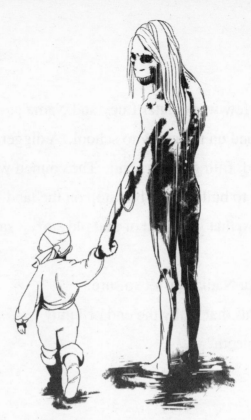

Nadia couldn't help shivering when she thought about her.

Her mum hadn't picked up Robbie from the party. And neither had Nadia.

But someone had.

Who?